THE NIGHT BEFORE THE NIGHT BEFORE CHRISTMAS

Kes Gray and Claire Powell

Hodder
Children's
Books

To Clement C. Moore

HODDER CHILDREN'S BOOKS
First published in Great Britain in 2018 by Hodder and Stoughton
This edition first published in 2021

Text copyright © Kes Gray, 2018
Illustrations copyright © Claire Powell, 2018
Slinky®

A CIP catalogue record for this book is available from the British Library.

ISBN: 9781 444 96005 1

1 3 5 7 9 10 8 6 4 2

Printed and bound in China

Hodder Children's Books
An imprint of Hachette Children's Group
Part of Hodder and Stoughton
Carmelite House
50 Victoria Embankment
London, EC4Y 0DZ

An Hachette UK Company
www.hachette.co.uk
www.hachettechildrens.co.uk

THE NIGHT BEFORE THE NIGHT BEFORE CHRISTMAS

Kes Gray and Claire Powell

Hodder Children's Books

'Twas the night before the night before Christmas
(That's Christmas Eve Eve),
and Santa was wiping
his brow on his sleeve.

Green elves were sewing,
blue elves were counting.
Red elves were carving,
the pressure was mounting.

23 DECEMBER

"Be quick!" Santa bellowed.
"There's so much to do!
My list is so long
it just isn't true!"

The elves put their heads down
and trebled their speed.
Ten billion presents
were what they would need.

Swingballs were tested,
puppets were strung.
Board games were boxed,
Slinkies were sprung.

Skateboards were oiled,
yo-yos were threaded.
Dollies were dressed,
teddies were teddied.

The workshop resounded
with elves hard at work.
There was no time to rest,
there was no time to shirk.

Santa looked down
and studied his list.
He was sure, he was sure
there was something he'd missed.

Aeroplanes? Bicycles?
Boomerangs? Drums?
Pogo sticks? Spinning tops?
Sugar mice? Sugarplums?

He ticked all the boxes
then turned with a jump.
Mrs Claus had arrived with
a plate, and the hump.

"Santa!" she grumbled.
"You've been asked, you've been told!
Now look what has happened –
your dinner's gone cold!"

Santa frowned crossly,
"I've no time to eat!
There's reindeer to ready
and deadlines to meet!"

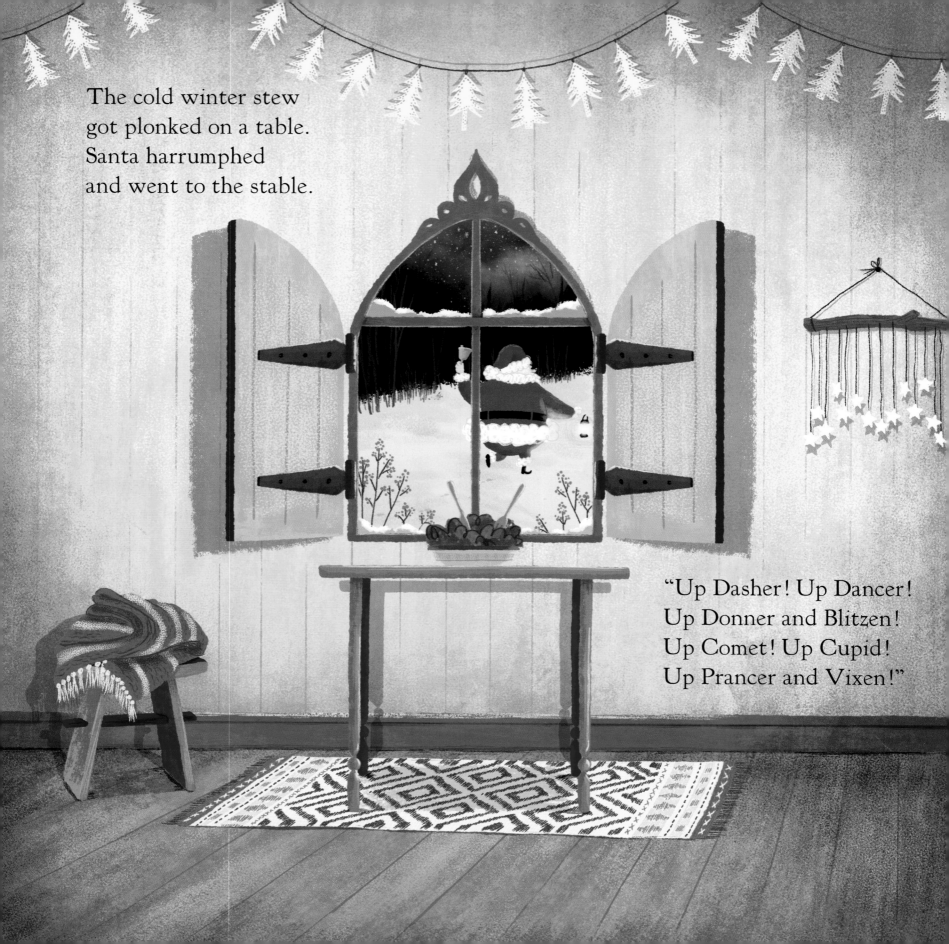

The cold winter stew
got plonked on a table.
Santa harrumphed
and went to the stable.

"Up Dasher! Up Dancer!
Up Donner and Blitzen!
Up Comet! Up Cupid!
Up Prancer and Vixen!"

The reindeer woke up
and climbed to their feet.
They had slept for a year
and needed to eat.

With reindeer refuelling
and time ticking by,
Santa ran out and
looked at the sky.

The North Star was twinkling,
snowflakes were falling.
Excitement was building,
Christmas was calling.

Back in the workshop
the shelves were now lined
with presents and gifts
of every kind.

Kites had been ribboned,
printing sets inked.
Spinning tops balanced,
tiddlies winked.

Toys had been tested,
batteries loaded.
Instruments tuned,
computer games coded.

"Remember!" said Santa,
"Our schedule is tight!"
The elves gave a nod
and worked through the night.

Popguns were loaded,
footballs inflated.
Candy canes twisted,
train sets tin-plated.

Dolls' clothes were folded,
annuals were printed.
Tangerines polished,
chocolate coins minted.

Santa thought hard
as the present piles grew.
He was sure there was something
he'd forgotten to do.

With take-off time now
only hours away,
he raced back outside
to inspect the sleigh.

The elves in hi-vis
had done Santa proud.
"Da dah!" they exclaimed
as they threw off the shroud.

Jet-washed and polished,
red, silver and gold,
the sleigh was a picture,
a joy to behold.

"Good job!" Santa shouted.
"Three cheers for you!
If I didn't know better,
I'd say it was new!"

Inside the workshop
the elves began clapping.
The presents were made,
it was time to get wrapping!

Paper was folded,
scissors were snipped.
Labels were written,
fountain pens dipped.

"Keep going!" cried Santa.
"It's Christmas Eve morning!
There's no time for breakfast
and no time for yawning!"

I guess you could say
that elves have the knack.
SEE! Ten billion presents . . .

. . . in one magic sack!

24
DECEMBER

"You've done it!" cheered Santa.
"We are done! We are there!
And not only that –
with minutes to spare!"

He ran through his list
and checked it all through.
What was it? What was it
he'd forgotten to do?

With a wave to his helpers,
he raced to the sleigh,
made himself comfy
and sat-navved the way.

"Giddy-up!"

Santa cried
with a nod and a wink.
The reindeer took off,
and were gone in a blink.

As dry leaves before
a spent hurricane slow,
so calmness returned
to the landscape below.

Chaos and mayhem
became stillness and peace,
until Mrs Claus ran out
in her best winter fleece.

"Santa!" she panted,
jumping the gate.
But Santa was gone;
Mrs Claus was too late.

"It's the same every year!"
she said with a wave.
"NICHOLAS, MY DEAR . . .